What's Michael?

The Ideal Cat

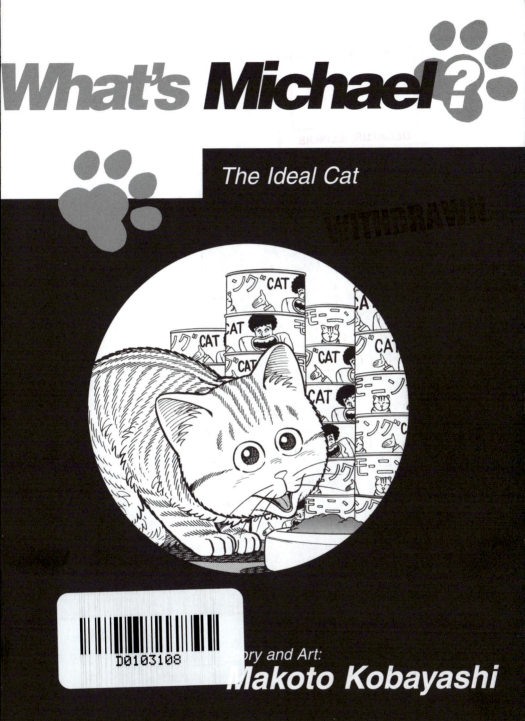

Story and Art:
Makoto Kobayashi

Translation:
Dana Lewis & **Lea Hernandez**

Dark Horse Manga™

Lettering and Retouch:
Digital Chameleon

publisher
Mike Richardson

series editor
Tim Ervin-Gore

series executive editor
Toren Smith for **Studio Proteus**

collection editor
Chris Warner

designer
Lani Schreibstein

art director
Lia Ribacchi

English-language version produced by
Studio Proteus and **Dark Horse Comics, Inc.**

What's Michael? Vol. IX: The Ideal Cat

This volume collects What's Michael? stories from
issues thirty-three through thirty-nine of the Dark
Horse comic-book series Super Manga Blast!

The artwork of this volume has been produced as
a mirror-image of the original Japanese
edition to conform to English-language standards.

Published by
Dark Horse Manga
A division of Dark Horse Comics, Inc.
10956 SE Main Street
Milwaukie, OR 97222

www.darkhorse.com

To find a comics shop in your area, call the
Comic Shop Locator Service toll-free at
1-888-266-4226

First edition: April 2004
ISBN: 1-59307-120-5

10 9 8 7 6 5 4 3 2 1

Printed in Canada

THE RULE

HEY!

GET ME SOME *TEA!*

SORRY DEAR, I *CAN'T.*

SEE...?

HE'S SLEEPING *SO* COMFORTABLY. HE'LL WAKE UP IF I MOVE.

YOU KNOW *THE RULE...* "NO DISTURBING MICHAEL!"

4

5

6

7

THE END

11

THE END

19

THE END

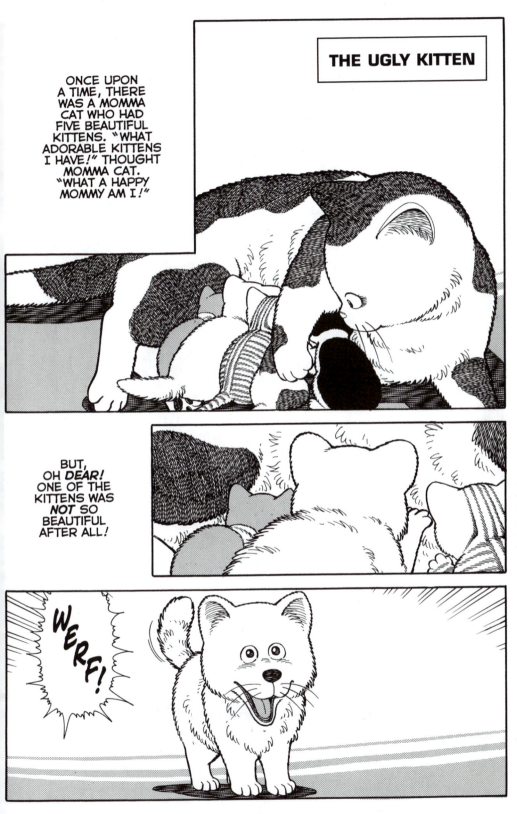

THE UGLY KITTEN

ONCE UPON A TIME, THERE WAS A MOMMA CAT WHO HAD FIVE BEAUTIFUL KITTENS. "WHAT ADORABLE KITTENS I HAVE!" THOUGHT MOMMA CAT. "WHAT A HAPPY MOMMY AM I!"

BUT, OH *DEAR!* ONE OF THE KITTENS WAS *NOT* SO BEAUTIFUL AFTER ALL!

WERF!

MOMMA CAT FROWNED, AND SAID:

"MY, YOU ARE AN *UGLY* KITTEN!"

ALL THE UGLY KITTEN'S SISTERS AND BROTHERS MADE FUN OF HIM.

NYA-NYAA! UHHHGLY!

UGLY KITTEN! MYAH!

BUT THE UGLY KITTEN DIDN'T SEEM TO MIND. HE JUST KEPT ON WAGGING HIS LITTLE TAIL AND LOVING HIS MOMMA CAT VERY MUCH!

WERF WHUF WHUF!

STOP BOUNCING AROUND LIKE THAT!

WHAP!

SADLY, MOMMA CAT ALWAYS SEEMED TO BE ANGRY WITH HIM.

ONE DAY, MOMMA CAT WAS TEACHING HER KITTENS HOW TO HUNT.

YOU HAVE TO LEARN TO MOVE WITHOUT MAKING A *SOUND!* UNDERSTAND?

YES, MAMA!

YES, MAMA!

MEWW!

MIAOW!

THE UGLY KITTEN FOLLOWED HIS SISTERS AND BROTHERS.

WHUF WHERF!

BUUUT...

⌇HAFF⌇
⌇HAFF⌇
⌇HAFF⌇

...HE WAS SO *HOT* HE THOUGHT HE'D *DIE!*

COME ON, LASSIE!

WHUFF! WHRUF!

EVEN THOUGH HE DIDN'T UNDER-STAND WHY, THE UGLY KITTEN'S FAVORITE TV SHOW WAS *LASSIE.*

25

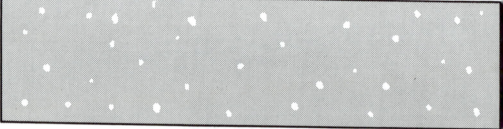

THE END

URASHIMA BEAR-O

"MUKASHI, MUKASHI,"* AS THE JAPANESE FOLK TALES GO, THERE WAS A YOUNG DOG NAMED "URASHIMA BEAR-O."

*: "ONCE UPON A TIME"

ONE DAY, URASHIMA BEAR-O HAPPENED UPON A GANG OF MONKEYS ON A BEACH, TORMENTING A HELPLESS KITTEN.

"HEY, YEW MONKEYS, GIT LOST!" SAID BEAR-O, BUT THE MONKEYS DIDN'T STOP. "IF YOU WANT US TO GO AWAY, GIVE US SOME MONEY," THEY SAID.

BEAR-O GAVE THE MONKEYS ALL THE COINS HE HAD, AND THE KITTEN WAS *SAVED!*

28

29

30

THE PERFECT SHOT

KENJI IWAHASHI. TWENTY-EIGHT. FREELANCE CAMERAMAN.

HE SEEKS *THE PERFECT SHOT* THAT WILL CAPTURE THE TRUE NATURE OF CATS, THEIR VERY *ESSENCE.*

TODAY, AS EVERY DAY, HE IS STALKING THE STREETS IN SEARCH OF HIS IDEAL SUBJECT-- *THE WILD ALLEY CAT!*

YES... THE *PER-FECT SHOT!*

AT TIMES LIKE THIS, IWAHASHI NEVER *PANICS* OR *PURSUES.*

....
....

HE PRETENDS NOT TO CARE. HE WALKS ON, *SURE* OF HIS QUARRY'S EVENTUAL RETURN.

38

"CAT WITH COOKIE"
PERFORMANCE ART
TAMAMI, 2003

THE END

THE THREE AMIGATOS

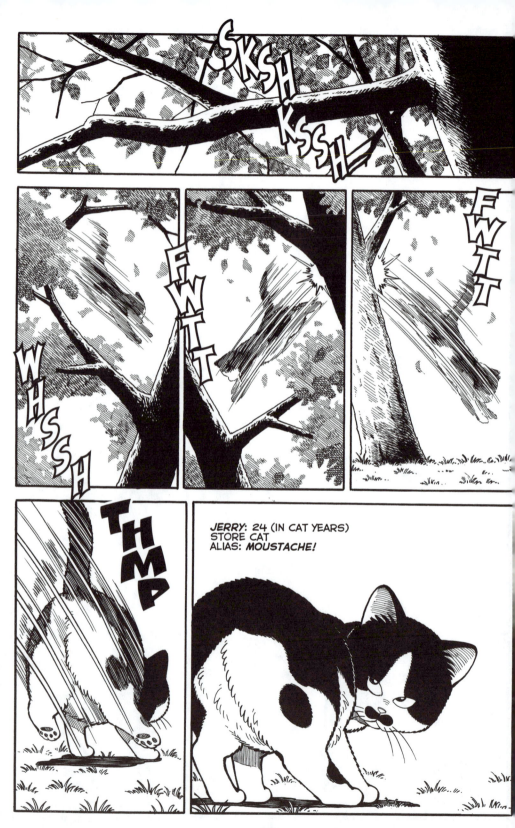

PLATO: 32 (IN CAT YEARS)
ALLEY CAT
ALIAS: *THE THINKER!*

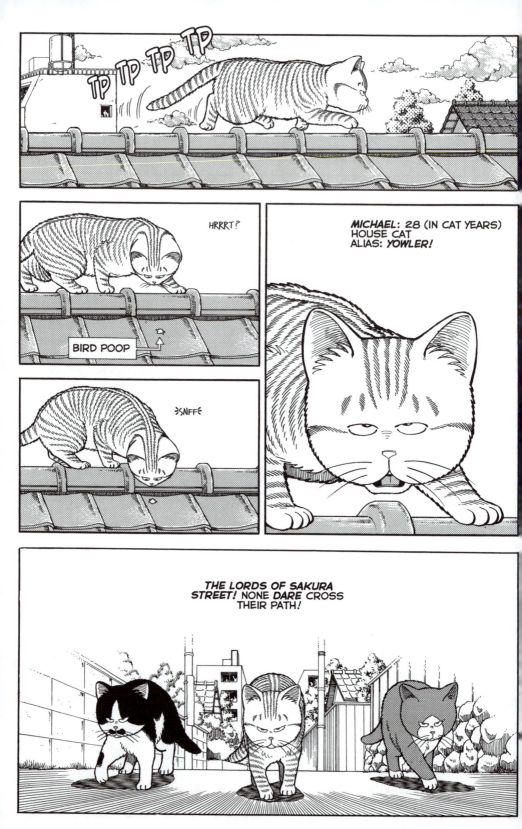

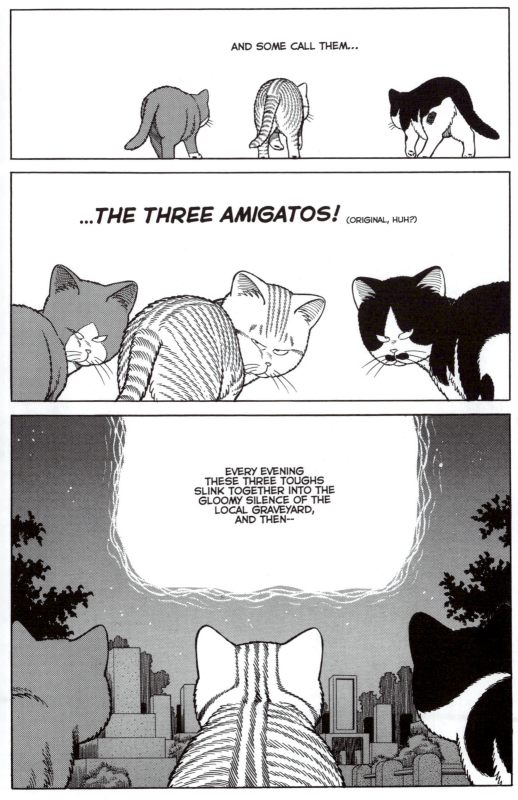

RETURN OF THE THREE AMIGATOS!

52

THE END

THE
COUNT
...!

HE FEARS
NEITHER
GARLIC NOR
CROSSES.

HE IS AN
*UNSTOP-
PABLE*
FIEND!

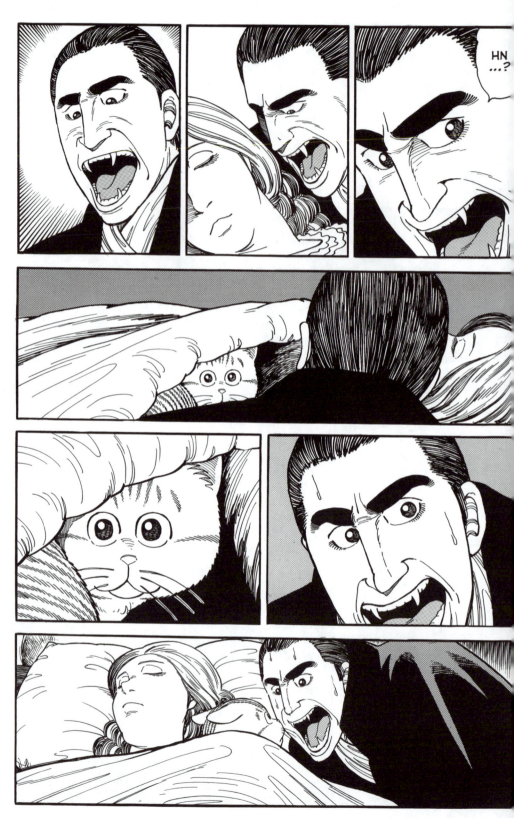

ER...UH... SORRY TO HAVE BOTHERED YOU.

ϟHFFϟ
ϟHAFFϟ

ϟHAFFϟ
ϟWHEW!ϟ

THE *COUNT*, *DEADLIEST* VAMPIRE OF THEM *ALL*, IS TERRIFIED--

--OF *CATS!* SO SCARED, IN FACT, THAT HIS JAW BECAME UNHINGED! (HOW EMBARRASSING!)

KER-POP!

unbowed
by rain,
unbowed
by wind...

unbowed
by rats,
unbowed by
roaches...

Upon your return from the fields, clean your paws before entering your home.

Always use the bathroom for your needs, and remember to flush.

Complain not of the sameness of your diet.

Complain not if you are alone for a weekend.

Clean up
after you
play.

Above all,
be the best
cat you
can be!

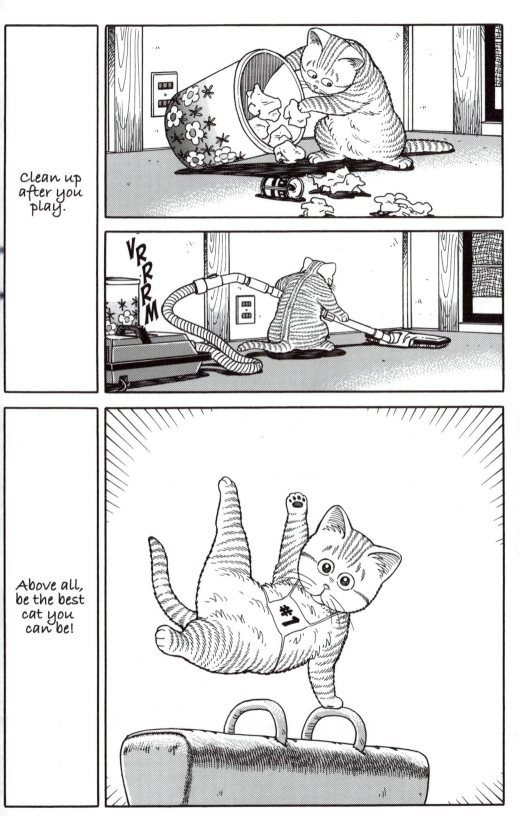

THE NABESHIMA AFFAIR

SAGA CASTLE, ON THE JAPANESE ISLAND OF KYUSHU.

A NOBLE SAMURAI...A LOYAL RETAINER!

RYUZOJI MATASABURO... SUMMONED THIS NIGHT TO THE CASTLE OF LORD NABESHIMA TO PLAY *MAH JONG.*

.....
.....

ETAK

PON!!*

AND *MAH JONG** ON THE LAST TILE! THAT'S TWO-THOUSAND BIG POINTS!

BWA HAW HAW HAW!

EH...?!

*THREE OF A KIND

*COMPLETED WINNING HAND

69

*A "STRAIGHT" RUN OF THREE

74

76

77

79

THE END

THE ALLEY CAT HUNTER

KENJI IWAHASHI, TWENTY-EIGHT. FREELANCE CAMERAMAN.

TODAY, AS EVERY DAY, HE STALKS THE CITY TO SHOOT... THE *WILD ALLEY CAT!*

!!

STILL SUSPICIOUS AT TEN FEET, EVEN WHEN I'M *SMALL!*

DAMN! WHY DIDN'T I BRING MY TELEPHOTO LENS...?

EH... ?

OH, *LOOKY* !

A *KITTY CAT!*

AREN'T YOU A *CUTIE!* ♥

I'VE GOT SOME KITTY TREATS IN MY PURSE. WANT TO GIVE HIM SOME...?

I DO, I DO! ♥

AWW, *LOOK!*

HE *LOVES* THEM!

.....
.....

HEH, HEH..!

NOW I'VE GOT YOU!

Maru, Male, Age Unknown

Meet Maru. My wife's family keeps Maru back at the family manse. And of course he's the model for Shinnosuke (Bear).

Now, I don't know what I've done to earn Maru's ire, but if I so much as approach him, even with a friendly smile on my face, he bares his teeth and snarls like crazy. And I wind up running full tilt for fifty meters or more

to get away. It's so bad that I have in fact never, not once, patted Maru on the head. My own daughter has yet to pet him.

Truth be told, though, I get barked at wherever I go.

So why the heck do dogs despise me so?

— Makoto Kobayashi